How Charlie, His Great-Great Grandfather, and SuperMax Saved the World

Stephen W. Peterson, M.D.
Antawon Y. Le Shiesh, Illustrator and Coauthor

DORRANCE
PUBLISHING CO
EST. 1920
PITTSBURGH, PENNSYLVANIA 15238

Dorrance Publishing Co
585 Alpha Drive
Suite 103
Pittsburgh, PA 15238
Visit our website at www.dorrancebookstore.com

ISBN: 978-1-6491-3424-0
eISBN: 978-1-6491-3556-8

How Charlie, His Great-Great Grandfather, and SuperMax Saved the World

Once upon a time, in the not-too-distant future, there lived a young boy named Charlie. Charlie lived in a strong house by the ocean with his parents. His mom and dad were special scientists who studied weather and climate changes. Climate changes were affecting all parts of everyday life more and more; his parents were studying how to live with these new changes.

The strong house was equipped with everything needed to measure winds, tides, all kinds of rain, snow or hail, earthquakes, and even volcanoes. They were trying to help people deal with increasingly difficult climate conditions.

Such houses were built all over the land so that dangerous climate events could be studied everywhere. Charlie had a super computer/robot that he called Max (short for SuperMax t28). Max was Charlie's playmate, companion, and teacher. It seemed that there wasn't anything Max didn't know—Max even understood the nature and importance of Charlie's parents' work. Since Charlie had to stay inside the strong house most of the time, Max was a perfect friend. Max was even considered part of the family. They had become pals.

One day, Charlie was outside looking off to the distance at yet another approaching storm when his mother called to him.

"Charlie, come in quickly! Another really big storm is coming fast."

Charlie hurried in. All through the night the winds howled as the storm grew stronger and stronger. After supper, his mom had run up to the roof to help his dad, who had been recording facts about the storm ever since the early afternoon. It was unusual for his father to be up there so long and to skip his dinner. This made Charlie nervous. He said to himself, "This must be a bad one."

Charlie turned to Max and said, "Is there anything we can do to help Mom and Dad with their work? They seem particularly worried and if these storms keep on getting worse and worse…is there anything that can stop these big storms?"

Max paused, lights flashing and programs buzzing. "Yes, Charlie, there is something we can try. First, your great-great-grandfather was a very important and powerful man. He was President of the United States and, they used to say, leader of the free world.

"In the year 2020 he had to make many crucial decisions, one being something they called clean energy. This did not seem so important back then, as there were many other problems. There was a great sickness that was happening at that time, and the people were frightened. Everyone was afraid to go out or to see anyone, and they all stopped working.

"Clean energy was something that had been talked about for many years before that, but not seriously. You see, before clean energy, machines ran on something called fossil fuels. They were found in the ground, where long ago plants and animals died and, afterward, turned into big layers of coal, oil, and gas. They had stored energy from ancient sunlight in them, and when they burned the energy was released, making heat and light appear again. They also produced a gas and tiny particles that made the earth get warm and made us sick.

"Fossil fuels were banned a few years ago and now we use new, clean ways to make energy from the wind and the sun. Back then, when your great-great-grandfather, Daniel Crump, was president, fossil fuels heated up the earth and made the air dirty. That's why we have big storms and air pollution today. We may be able to convince President Crump to stop using so much fossil fuel 60 years ago and start using clean energy back when he was our leader."

"How can we do that?" asked Charlie. "That was 60 years ago."

"I'm glad you asked," said Max. "It happens that the t2 series SuperMax computers have a special technology—one that we will only use under certain circumstances, that is, for limited time travel. We can go back as far as 80 to 100 years ago and return safely. The reason we don't talk about it is that people could use it the wrong way—and once you change history it affects everything that comes after, for better or for worse. I would say this is a good reason to go back, and it just so happens your great-great-grandpa is someone who can make an important difference."

Charlie thought for a moment. "Couldn't we be killed?" Suddenly his excitement turned to fear.

"You mean you, or me?" said Max. "No. The real danger is making things worse, but I think we will make things way better."

Charlie realized he must do something, if only to help his parents. "Okay, what do we do?"

"First," said Max, "there is a special metal that makes what we are about to do—time travel—possible. It has very specific properties that any beginning scientist would recognize. Sixty years ago scientists were trying to make this metal called Zircontron-3. I will form a chunk of this into a medal, and I will put your great-great-grandfather's face on it with some nice words of praise. Not only will he like this, but it will give him the idea of what he is supposed to do to change the future. See? Next, you gather some old family photographs—some more recent and some really old ones. The photographs will prove who you are. President Crump could be very suspicious because people were always trying to fool him. He loves and trusts his children and grandchildren, though, so when he knows who you are, he will listen to you. Now you gather the pictures while I charge my batteries.... And don't tell your parents what we're up to—they may be too afraid to let us go."

Soon all the preparations were done, and Charlie slipped into SuperMax's special compartment.

Max whirred, blinked, and they were off to the past.

In what seemed like only a few seconds, Charlie noticed the whirring sound winding down, and they were there—in President Crump's office! When he opened the hatch to Max's compartment, he saw his great-great-grandfather and two other people standing by his desk.

All had startled looks on their faces.

Charlie got up and quickly said, "Hi, President Crump! I'm your great-great grandson , Charlie, and I have come to ask for your help. I also brought along some things to prove I am who I say I am.

President Crump was speechless, as were the two friends he had been talking to.

"First, I want to show you this." Charlie pulled the medal out of his pocket and gave it to the President.

As the president looked at the medal, Charlie said, "It's made of a special metal. Your scientists are trying to make this metal. It's Zircontron-3. You could ask your scientist to look at it." (Max had very slyly planned his time of arrival for when the president was talking to his favorite scientist on the very topic.)

The president started to hand the medal over to his favorite scientist when he noticed his image on it.

"Why is my face on this medallion?" the president asked.

"When Max made it," Charlie replied, "he hoped you would consider making policy changes about our use of energy. He thought you might change the thinking in the United States about using fossil fuels and switch to clean energy. So the medal commemorates your part in taking an unpopular step in working on this problem."

(the back of the medal reads:

> The Great Crump
>
> Whose Keen Foresight
>
> Convinced the World
>
> Clean Energy Is Good
>
> For the Planet)

"You see," said Charlie, "you were the first great leader to rise above the politics of this situation and to see the potential danger. But, of course, the medal won't exist if you don't stand behind clean energy."

The president handed the medal to his top scientist.

"Wow," said she, "this is something really different and important! I've never seem this metal before!"

"Max told me that it is similar to what helped us travel through time," said Charlie.

Then he gave President Crump his folder with the pictures in it. The president spent a few minutes looking through them, clearly impressed with their authenticity.

"The reason I came here," said Charlie, "is to ask you about climate change and the need for clean energy. Sixty years from now we will be living in a world with almost constant dangerous weather…that is where I came from. If you don't work with other world leaders to fix this problem, I will have to live this way, and I'm not sure how long people can live in a world like this or worse."

The president put the folder of pictures on his desk and looked at the medal again. "Remarkable! What a brave kid you are to take this on…you are a TRUE CRUMP! Your great-great-grandpops will call together world leaders and get on this problem right away!

The metal in this medal should be proof enough for them. What a fantastic person you are, I am very proud of you!"

Max was getting impatient; he was whirring and blinking again. "Charlie, we need to get back! Remember, we only have a limited amount of time here!"

"Oh, right," said Charlie. "I'm really glad I met you, Great-Great-Grandpa Daniel! The history books had no idea who you really are, but I think they will now!"

The president thought to himself, *I wonder if that kid will be president himself, one day….*"

Charlie waved goodbye and jumped back into Max. They were on their way in a flash.

It seemed to take longer to get back. Charlie was anxious to see if anything had actually changed at his home.

"Why are we going so slowly?" complained Charlie.

"Patience, Charlie," said Max. "My batteries are a little low; we'll get there when we get there."

When they finally did arrive, Charlie crawled out and found himself on the front lawn of a beautiful stone house. Before he had a chance to worry, his mother and dad appeared at the front door with their arms outstretched, greeting and hugging their son.

"What a brave thing you did, son! It is as if we always knew you did this, and all that happened before was a terrible nightmare," his dad exclaimed.

"And I'm glad I didn't know about your plan," said his mother, "because I never would have let you go and then, well, this wonderful world could not have existed!" She was holding back tears of joy at seeing her son safely home again.

"What a beautiful world," said Charlie. "President Crump was a real hero! And Max knew just the right moment to land in the Oval Office! He's the other hero!"

Then Max said, "Charlie, without you, it couldn't have been done. You are the real hero!"

Max rolled into the new house behind Charlie and his happy parents, and they all had some lemonade and cookies for a treat. By the way, they all lived happily ever after in a world without big storms and dangerous weather.

CPSIA information can be obtained
at www.ICGtesting.com
Printed in the USA
BVHW060959151220
595411BV00002B/19